Alicia's
Mindfulness

AuthorHouse™
1663 Liberty Drive
Bloomington, IN 47403
www.authorhouse.com
Phone: 833-262-8899

Because of the dynamic nature of the Internet, any web addresses or links contained in this book may have changed since publication and may no longer be valid. The views expressed in this work are solely those of the author and do not necessarily reflect the views of the publisher, and the publisher hereby disclaims any responsibility for them.

Any people depicted in stock imagery provided by Getty Images are models, and such images are being used for illustrative purposes only.
Certain stock imagery © Getty Images.

This book is printed on acid-free paper.

ISBN: 978-1-4918-3623-1 (sc)
ISBN: 978-1-4918-3624-8 (e)

Library of Congress Control Number: 2013920973

Print information available on the last page.

Published by AuthorHouse 09/21/2023

authorHOUSE®

Alicia's
Mindfulness

Written by
Raul Salazar & Grover Clark

Illustrator by
Susan Shorter

Introduction

In 2012, before I attended a meditation course, my brother-in-law, Grover Clark, commented that someone should write a meditation book for children. He suggested that it would help if meditation was introduced at a young age. This triggered something in me. After a meditation course, I wrote *Alicia's Mindfulness*. That was the beginning of the process to complete this book.

This book was initially intended for children. Due to the complexity and the abstract nature of the topic, I came to the understanding that small children may have difficulty grasping some of the concepts. With that said, I feel this book is appropriate for all abstract-thinking ages. I hope this book creates a welcoming environment to introduce a subject as complex as meditation.

This book is intended to shed light on the theory and practice of meditation through a storytelling approach. This book is *not* intended to be an instructional manual. Thank you and enjoy. Metta (an expression of loving kindness to all).

Chapter 1

Morality

The day welcomed Alicia as she stirred from her rest. Although she wasn't aware of it, she was going to start a journey that would deeply change her life. While Alicia was walking to the playground, she noticed an army of ants and stopped to watch them for a moment. Later, she noticed a bee flying from flower to flower.

The ants and the bees have a role in life, she thought before asking herself, *what's my purpose?* She didn't know the answer and kept on walking.

At the playground, Alicia observed a flock of birds flying in formation and realized that there was a natural intelligence and harmony in the world. She felt a deep emotional reaction.

The next morning, she heard a soft buzzing sound outside her window and saw a beautiful hummingbird. Its shiny feathers were glittering as it zipped about gracefully.

As Alicia opened the window to get a better look, she heard the hummingbird say, "Hi, my name is Koe-Soes."

She was so startled she almost didn't hear the tiny voice. She focused her concentration and heard, "Are you Alicia? I'm Koe-Soes."

Alicia was shocked that a bird was talking to her. She cautiously replied, "Yes, I'm Alicia.... But, how do you know my name, and how can you speak?"

Koe-Soes said, "Mother Nature sent me to guide you. She said she heard your desire to know your purpose. Mother speaks to those people who have a pure heart and a willing spirit. Mother Nature knows you are ready."

Koe-Soes continued. "I am here to teach you how to better understand your purpose in life, through the practice of meditation. Meditation is the path to insight and wisdom. You will learn to focus your mind with unconditional acceptance. Meditation will help you experience what is happening in your life with nonattachment and peace of mind. You're welcome to come outside so we can start your practice."

Although bewildered, Alicia understood Koe-Soes and smiled. She was unsure but also delighted, and so she went outside.

As they met in the yard, Koe-Soes explained, "In order to fulfill your purpose, you must have a calm and steady mind. The first step is to live a good life."

"What does a good life mean?" Alicia asked.

"It means to live a moral life. Please understand that you need to live a life of honor without harming yourself or others. Always treat others like you would like to be treated, with compassion and kindness. This is how to live a good life," Koe-Soes answered. "All life is sacred and interconnected. You will come to understand that to do harm to others is to harm yourself.

"You see, Alicia, you need a calm mind to experience reality as it is. Continuous mental chit-chat creates disturbance. When your mind is disturbed, you become unbalanced and are unable to experience the natural harmony of the world. To quiet the mind is to live in peace. That is your purpose. This is the first step on your path."

Chapter 2

Concentration

"Remember when I introduced myself and you couldn't hear me?" Koe-Soes asked.

Alicia nodded yes.

"What you did was focus the attention of your hearing sensation," Koe-Soes continued. "You have several senses through which you experience the world. The main senses are: seeing, smelling, tasting, hearing, feeling, and involved thinking or consciousness."

"Con ... shus ... ness?" Alicia questioned.

"I know *consciousness* is a big word, but it simply means awareness," explained Koe-Soes. "It helps you understand the meaning of things. The universe speaks to you through your senses. That is how you get information. Something from the outside world touches one of your senses, and the mind recognizes it and decides if it's good or bad. This creates a body sensation, and a mental reaction is formed. This happens spontaneously and is automatic."

Alicia scratched her head. "Wow, that's a lot."

Koe-Soes clarified. "The mental reaction is an emotion that is connected to a body sensation or a feeling. When you have an emotion, it turns into a sensation in the body; the same thing happens the other way around. Feelings, or body sensations, create emotions. Whenever there is a thought or emotion, there is a sensation in the body. To experience this process firsthand is a function of meditation."

This was a lot for Alicia to understand, and she had a puzzled look on her face.

"Yes, it's a lot to understand," Koe-Soes told Alicia. "When you see something, your sense of sight starts to work. When you smell something, your sense of smell starts to work. When you eat or drink something, your sense of taste starts to work.

When you hear a voice or a noise, your hearing sense starts to work. When you feel something on your skin, your sense of touch starts to work. And when you have a thought, your mind sense starts to work."

Koe-Soes continued. "This is how the outside world touches your senses. This first step is *identification*. It's when your mind says, 'Something has happened, and I know what that is.' The second step is *evaluation* when your mind says whether it's good or bad. The third step is a *physical reaction, a body sensation, a feeling*. This is a natural job of the mind and body to let us know what's happening. But the fourth part, when the mind creates a *mental reaction*, is when you can affect a change. This is where you are in charge. Bringing your attention to the present moment is how you train your mind. Awareness without attachment is the key to transforming your life. Your goal is to learn how to be aware of your body and not identify yourself with the feelings. Present moment awareness with nonattachment brings you in harmony with life."

It was clear Alicia was still very overwhelmed with all of this.

"I know it's a lot of new stuff," Koe-Soes said. "Let's go find a safe and quiet place to learn to meditate."

They found a nice spot in Alicia's backyard under a shady tree. Koe-Soes began to guide Alicia. "Sit down, keep your back straight, place your hands comfortably in your lap, and close your eyes. Bring your attention to your nose. Can you feel the breath touching where it enters your nose?"

Alicia mumbled. "Uh-huh."

Koe-Soes confirmed. "Good. By focusing your mind on a small area of your body, you develop your concentration. The longer you can keep doing this, the stronger your mind will become. The goal is to keep your focus from moment to moment, continuously. Let's see how long you can do this before you become distracted."

It only took Alicia a few moments before she started to think about how silly all this was, and then she realized that she wasn't keeping her focus.

Koe-Soes sensed Alicia's struggle. "Yeah, it's hard work! But keep bringing your attention back. Don't get upset or frustrated. Accept this moment as it is. Gently refocus your attention."

They practiced together for several days, and Alicia noticed a steady improvement in her concentration.

One day, at the end of meditation, Koe-Soes observed the changes in Alicia. "You are making progress. You are training your mind to be in the present moment, not daydreaming or remembering. You want pure awareness—just watch, just witness. No reactions. A calm mind."

Alicia excitedly opened her eyes and said, "I get it! I can use my breath to sharpen my mind, so I can cut through the daydreams or the memories!"

They continued practicing, and Alicia became very strong at focusing her mind. She began feeling sensations all over her body but kept her attention on her breathing.

Chapter 3

Wisdom

Koe-Soes said, "Observing your breath without reacting teaches us equanimity. *Equanimity* means to have a calm mind because you are aware of and accept the present moment. This how you become mindful."

"E-quan-im-it-y, eee-quannn-imm-it-y, equanimity—wow, that's a hard word!" Alicia struggled.

Koe-Soes explained, "To become equanimous, you need to train your mind to watch your breath without reaction, without attachment. Recall when you were paying attention to your breath and just experiencing yourself without judgment, labeling, thoughts, or distractions, That's what it's like to be equanimous—pure awareness and experience."

Koe-Soes continued. "During your meditation, keep your mind strong and focused on your breath. As your mind becomes calmer, you will be able to focus deeper. Consistency is the key to success. When you are equanimous, you are changing how your mind works. When you are aware and equanimous, you are teaching the 'thinking part' of your mind and the 'feeling part' of your mind to work together. You are training your mind to watch and not react—to be equanimous. You are changing how your mind works—from a reacting mind to an accepting mind. When you react, it's kind of like twisting a swing in circles. Have you ever done that?"

Alicia smiled and said, "Yeah, I really like it. When I let go, I untwist and go around and around. It's fun."

"I'm glad you understand," Koe-Soes said, "because twisting a swing is just what your mind does when it reacts. It twists and twists and twists. You are doing two things when you watch with equanimity. You're bringing your mind to focus, and you are training your mind not to react, just watch. And when you stop twisting the swing, what happens?"

Alicia exclaimed. "You get untangled!"

14

"That's right," said Koe-Soes. "Watching instead of reacting is how you untangle your mind. You are training your mind to see reality as it is, not as you would like it to be."

"This practice will bring peace and harmony to your life. This is wisdom. This is mindfulness."

"This is mindfulness," Alicia repeated. "I will just experience my breath and be eeequaan-imm-ous ... equanimous. That's it."

"Understand that what you are experiencing is temporary, and it will go away. Another experience will come along, because new information is always coming in from the world. This is impermanence. Impermanence is the way nature works. It means that things are always changing. Everything in the universe is constantly changing. This part of your training is very important. This is how you can stop reacting. When the mind reacts, it does one of two things: it can like it and want more of it, or it can dislike it and want it to go away. And because we can't always get what we want, we suffer. Have you ever really wanted something and thought you would be totally happy if you received it? But after you've had it for a while, you are not satisfied with it?"

Alicia smiled and said, "Yes, I do that all the time."

Koe-Soes explained. "You are training your mind to observe and not react. This is how you change the way your mind works. Wisdom is the knowledge you will gain through pure, direct experience.

"Now you have the techniques to build your daily practice. Make sure you keep your mind focused during meditation, be equanimous, and understand that everything is changing. Keep your mindfulness practice throughout the day. Remember to treat others as you would like to be treated. May all beings live in harmony; may all beings know peace. Blessings to you, Alicia. Everything in the universe has to change. Our time together has ended. Mother Nature has asked me to help someone else now."

And just like that, Koe-Soes flickered, and something changed in her. She became a beautiful, natural hummingbird and flew away. The powers that Mother Nature blessed her with were gone.

After Koe-Soes's visit, Alicia worked hard on her mindfulness practice and maintained her daily meditation. She came to understand how her emotional attachment to her changing thoughts was the starting point of suffering. This realization guided her to explore deeper levels of reality and develop her goals of peace of mind with present moment awareness and equanimity.

The end.

Acknowledgements

To all who have supported my meditation practice and offered input or helped me

edit Alicia's Mindfulness, thank you!

Grover Clark, brother-in-Law, great spiritual soul, and fundamental inspiration in my life, I honor you. For your unconditional guidance and support of my meditation path, thank you. Thank you for co-writing Alicia's Mindfulness.

Florita Sheldon, I feel blessed to know you. I am honored to work with you on the Orange County Alopecia Areata Support Group. Thank you for all of your help developing and editing Alicia's Mindfulness. Your participation was essential. I also would like to express my gratitude to your daughter Sophia for her input on the book.

Jeffrey Hancuff, my dhamma brother, thank you for your expertise and thoughts with the meditation technique.

Michael Weahkee, Zuni, life guide coach, and great friend, I admire your professionalism and strength. Thank you for molding my path in education, career and for expanding my understanding of the American Indian/Native American ways. I'm a better person because of you.

Ane Marie McDonald, instant friend, educator and spiritual nurturer, your direction revealed to me that which I was capable of accomplishing. Bless you. I cherish you.

Therese Gonzalez, Thank you for your input, encouragement and support with Alicia's Mindfulness. You have helped me grow as a human and professional.

Gloria Alicia Clark, loving and kind beautiful sister, cooking teacher, model of strength, and upcoming Vipassana student, you have validated my path. Thank you.

Xavier Salazar, humorous, great, older brother, endless caretaker and loving kind father. I admire and cherish you. Thank you for everything.

Elizabeth Lara - O'Rourke, Hupa/Yurok/Chilula, great friend, spiritual inspiration, and Healer, I have reflected my spiritual life after yours, Healer. For shaping my holistic world view and guiding my journey into the American Indian/Native American community, I am immensely grateful.

Leticia "Bunz" Tarango, Navajo, my great friend, we have the same twisted sense of humor. Thank you for your involvement in this book.

Koe-Soes Vigil, Hupa/Yurok, excellent friend, you're namesake is the inspiration for Alicia's hummingbird guide. For your deep connection to this book, I thank you.

Lucy Allen, Luceno Band of Mission Indians, blessed elder and committed supporter, you have shown me fortitude and wisdom. For your contribution in my success in anything, thank you.

Becky Garrow, your enthusiastic and positive regard of Alicia's Mindfulness inspired me to follow up and work hard. Thank you.

Karen Young, thank you for your support and assistance in developing this book through the perspective of a mental health therapist.

Stacie, Kwaku, Barron and Carver Oppong, your family is beautiful. Thank you for being great friends. You have helped me understand the medical perspective of mindfulness. Thank you for having Barron and Carver field-test the book.

Georgianna Hubble Lord, cherished childhood friend, I have learned so much from you. For having your kids, Julia Rangel, Jayden Lord, and Jonah Lord, field test my book, and for your invaluable influence in pursing publication for this book, I give thanks to you and your family.

To the American Indian/Native American community and my Indian friends, your impressions on my life have inspired this narrative, which follows Indian/Native American oral story telling history. Thank you.